It was a busy day in Greendale. Peter Fogg was dashing off to do the milking, on his motorbike, and Ted was on his way, in his lorry, to mend a hole in a roof.

Pat was out early as well, but *he* was going slowly! He had such a load of parcels today! Some of them wanted to escape. Miss Hubbard found one that had got away, lying on the ground.

"Oh - a parcel - now I wonder who . . .? Well, there's an address on it - I'd better give it to Pat."

Pat met her round the next corner.

"Morning! Parcel for you! Sorry I'm a bit late!"

"And I have one for you!" said Miss Hubbard. "I found it lying in the street."

"Dear me, Miss Hubbard, I must have dropped it. Thank you! My bag is so full today!"

"Goodness me, Pat, I hope you'll take more care. It's taken a bit of a knock. And I don't think Mrs Crockett will be too pleased to get a *muddy* parcel."

"Now don't you worry, Miss Hubbard, I'll give it a wipe before I deliver it. It's very nice of you to pick it up for me. I've never seen so many parcels in all my days. It's a real worry, getting round the village with them. I can't use the van in these narrow yards, you know."

Pat went on his way.
"One thing - my bag gets lighter as I go along! Soon be done, now."
At last, his bag was empty.
"I'm glad that lot's finished!"

But, when he went back to the post office, there was another pile of parcels waiting for him.

"What's that? Not another load?"

"Oh, Pat, I'm so sorry," said Mrs Goggins. "I don't know where they're all coming from!"

"It's worse than Christmas!" said Pat. "What's going on? All the parcels in the world seem to be coming to Greendale!"

"Just take as many as you can," said Mrs Goggins, "then come back for another lot. That's the only way! Little by little - you'll manage."

"This bag's such a weight - it's giving me a sore back, and I need arms like a gorilla!"

There were so many parcels in Pat's van that there was hardly any room for Jess.

"Now then, Jess, where are you going to sit? Shove up a bit, and make room for another parcel. One of these days, there won't be enough room for *me* to get in," said Pat, "then *you'll* have to drive the van, Jess!"

Pat squeezed in somehow, and went on his way.

The first stop today was
Thompson Ground.
Sam's van was ahead of Pat,
and there was Dorothy,
looking at a big glossy catalogue,
full of coloured pictures.

There was a pile of parcels for her.
"Now, then, Dorothy," said Pat.
"Just look at this lot! All for you!"
"Oooh, Pat, how nice!" said Dorothy.
"I was hoping they'd come today."
"I can't say I was! I've had a
huge load of parcels today. It's like
ten Christmases all at once! Where
are they all coming from?"
"It's this here catalogue, Pat,"
said Sam. "It's got *everything* in!
All the things I can't fit into my van!
Folks love it! They're ordering
stuff like mad, and they all come
through the post."
"Now I see!" said Pat.
"Skirts and blouses!" said Dorothy.
"TVs and videos!" said Sam.
"Pots and pans!" said Dorothy.
"Oh, help!" said Pat.
"Cheerio!" said Sam.

Pat was on his way.

"Nay, Jess!" he said. "It's going to get worse. I don't know what we're going to do. It'll be beds and wardrobes, next."

At Ted Glen's, Ted was looking out for Pat. There was the biggest pile of parcels for Ted.

Pat staggered up to the door with them, dropping them as he went. "Ooooops!"

"Hey up, Pat!" said Ted, as he caught the flying parcels.

"What this, then? A new sort of air-mail?"

"Sorry about that,
Ted, but I just can't cope.
Everybody's gone mad,
ordering every mortal thing
from that catalogue of Sam's."
"Well, you'll have to move with the
times, Pat. Come up to date! It's no good
staggering round with a bag of parcels,
breaking your arm."
"I can't get the van round these lanes and yards
in the villages," said Pat.
"Nay, Pat, you want a high-tech solution. I'll have
a think about it. I'm sure I can come up with something."
"I hope you can," said Pat, "before I get squashed
under a pile of parcels. Cheerio!"

The next day, Major Forbes was on the look-out for a parcel he had sent for, when he spotted Pat, behind a high pile of parcels!

"By Jove!" barked the Major, "there's my parcel, right at the bottom! I'll just –"

"Oh!!! Help!" yelled Pat, as the Major tugged his parcel out, making all the other parcels tumble to the ground.

"It's all right, Pat," said the Major, "I've got it! Bye bye!"

Round the corner, Doctor Gilbertson was chatting to Dorothy
Thompson . . .

". . . and I was just saying I could do with a new car, when
Sam showed me that catalogue of his."

"Ooh, yes, it's wonderful," said Dorothy. "There's everything in it."

Pat walked straight into Doctor Gilbertson, and his parcels went
flying again!

"Whoa!" he shouted.

"Oh, help!" said Dorothy. "What's —?"

Doctor Gilbertson helped Pat up and said,

"Now, Pat, you don't need to be so rough about delivering the mail! I'll be having some broken legs to mend."

"I'm sorry, Doctor," said Pat. "It's this mail-order madness that's come over the whole of Greendale."

"Well I think the Royal Mail should do something about it," said the doctor. "It's not good for your health - or for ours, if it comes to that! What if I order a new car? I'll put a word in with your boss, in Pencaster."

"Well, I hope somebody does something!" said Pat. "A new car? Now that would make a super parcel! I don't think *that* would go in my bag."

The next day, it was time to call on Ted again.
He was too busy to look out for Pat.
    "More parcels!"
    "Have a look at this, Pat," said Ted.
"I think it'll solve your problem.
The Mark One, Super Speed,
Postal Scooter! Just what the modern
postman needs in the age of mail-order!"
    "It looks grand, Ted.
I like the parcel-box in front.
Is there room for a cat?"
    "There's room for everything.
Why don't you try it out?
Have a test-run."
    "Well, I don't know how you've
done it so quickly. I'll just try the seat.
What are you doing, Ted?
You're not starting the engine are you?
How do you turn it off?"

But Pat's question
was too late.
The Postal Scooter
shot out of the workshop
door, taking Pat with it.
"Ohhhhhh!"

Pat shot down the hill, through an open gate, into a field,
and crashed into a haystack.

"Are you all right, Pat?" panted Ted, when he found Pat. "I think
it needs a bit of fettling before you use it for real, a few adjustments . . ."

"Ermm - yes, Ted, quite a few," said Pat, picking himself out of
the hay. "Like, well, putting brakes on it?"

A few days later, Mrs Pottage was talking to Mrs Goggins outside the post office . . .

"That Pat, he makes a great racket, these days, when he goes round with the village post."

"Aye, well, it is a bit noisy," said Mrs Goggins, "but he certainly gets round with the parcels, now."

"But he seems to think he's in some sort of race!" said Mrs Pottage.

There was a loud bang, and Pat came whizzing along the village street on his Postal Scooter.

Mrs Goggins and Mrs Pottage jumped into the post office doorway for safety.

"I see what you mean!" said Mrs Goggins.

PC Selby was having a quiet stroll, when Pat shot into view. He jumped into Mr Pringle's garden. Pat shot in at the open gate, and out the other end.

"My goodness," said Mr Pringle, "Pat *is* in a hurry! Must be a terribly urgent telegram - but why did he come through here?"

The steep hills slowed Pat down a bit, but only when he was going *up* them!

Pat tumbled off at the bottom of one hill, with parcels scattered all about.

George Lancaster came along and helped to gather them up, saying, "Here you are Pat. Are you trying to sow them?"

PC Selby was looking for Pat in the post office.

"Morning, Mrs Goggins. Can I have a quiet word?" he said.

"I thought you might be popping in," said Mrs Goggins.

"I've had complaints. It's this high-speed postman of ours."

"Poor old Pat," said Mrs Goggins. "He's only trying to do his job."

"Right enough, but he's making a dickens of a racket, and endangering life and limb."

"Let me have a word with Pat," said Mrs Goggins. "I know he'll listen to me. No need for him to be in trouble."

"I'll leave it to you, then," said PC Selby. "A word to the wise, eh? Thanks. See you, Mrs Goggins !"

Pat came in, a minute later.

"Was that PC Selby just now?" he said.

"Yes, it was, Pat, and it was you he was talking about. He's taken your name and address."

"He knows it! We went to school together."

"Never mind that. He's really cross with you. Been causing a lot of noise and danger, haven't you? Tearing round on that scooter-thing!"

"But - how else can I deliver all the parcels on time, if they keep on coming like this?"

"Well, Pat, just as it happens, there's a parcel for *you* today - it's a big one; have a look in it, you never know what it might be."

"For me? Well - who can be sending one for me? I certainly haven't ordered anything from that blooming catalogue."

Pat unwrapped the huge parcel.

"Well, bless me - it's - it's - one of those trolleys - a proper postal-trolley - I saw one when I went to London on that trip! Well, this should be a bit of all right. Let's get it loaded up . . ."

Off Pat went, proudly wheeling his postal-trolley.
He met the Reverend Timms.
  "What do you reckon to this, Reverend?" said Pat.
  "Wonderful! Ah, Pat, you see, the Lord will provide."
  "No, it came from the Royal Mail in Pencaster,"
said Pat. "It's to help me deal with all these parcels."
      "And it's nice and quiet,"
said the Reverend Timms.
      "Just the thing for our peaceful
corner of the world. Bye, Pat!"

Doctor Gilbertson was out shopping.
"Morning, Doctor Gilbertson!"
"Hello, Pat. I like your
new trolley! Nice and
quiet. Holds more
parcels, too."
"It'll save me
going off *my*
trolley," said
Pat, "I can
tell you!"

Pat went, whistling cheerfully, up the village street. Jess rode
amongst the parcels and packets; he loved it. "Come on, Jess," said Pat.
"You can give *me* a ride when we've done."

But Jess wasn't at all sure
about that. Who ever heard
of a cat pulling a trolley?